When you create
do you have th[e]
out in advance or do you allow
their personalities to drive their
actions (and thus the plot)?

MUSIC

HISTORY

OR A PLAY ABOUT GREEKS AND SNCC IN 1963

SANDRA SEATON

MUSIC HISTORY
or A Play About Greeks and SNCC in 1963

2015 Edition

The author wishes to give special thanks to Charles Payne, whose powerful book *I've Got the Light of Freedom: The Organizing Tradition and the Mississippi Freedom Struggle* (University of California Press, 1997) was an invaluable resource in writing *Music History*.

Note on use of music in play:

The playwright prefers that productions use the music listed in the script. It is the responsibility of the producer to make the necessary arrangements with the holders of music copyrights for royalties. If alternative music is desired, the playwright's original intent should be kept in mind. Alternative choices must be approved by the playwright or the playwright's representative prior to production.

CAST

WALTER DANIELS: African-American, 24, a grad
student in Political Science. Fraternity member. Part-time
jazz pianist. Wears tailored clothes in a style made popular
by Miles Davis.

ETTA BRADSHAW: African-American, 19, a sophomore,
undergrad. Pledge in Pi Lambda, an African American
sorority. Her clothes are a cross between Jackie Kennedy
and French ingénue, a style gleaned from magazines and
French New Wave films.

FRANK: Walter's fraternity brother

MONICA: Etta's Pi Lambda pledge sister

FEEZIE: Etta's Pi Lambda pledge sister

SHIRLEY: Etta's Pi Lambda pledge sister

SOROR BANKS: Pi Lambda active. (offstage voice)

MRS. DANIELS: Walter's mother (offstage voice)

MR. DANIELS: Walter's father (offstage voice)

MRS. BRADSHAW: Etta's mother (offstage voice)

MRS. HURLEY: Owner of rental house (offstage voice)

NOTE: In the November 2010 Michigan State University
production, there was a cast of 9 actors. The actors playing
Mr. and Mrs. Daniels and Mrs. Bradshaw appeared on the

side of the stage in a well of light; Soror Banks remained offstage. Mrs. Bradshaw and Soror Banks were played by the same actor. Mrs. Daniels and Mrs. Hurley were played by the same actor.

SETTING: The living room of an apartment on the University of Illinois campus.

TIME: Late Spring 1963.

ACT ONE

SCENE ONE

Walter and Etta are sitting on Walter's sofa. There are several windows on the wall in back of them. A record player sits on the floor near the sofa. Etta is wearing a black sheath dress and heels. Walter wears Ivy League shirt and pants.

ETTA: Every other Saturday.

WALTER: **(slightly teasing)** Every other Saturday? Why not every Saturday?

ETTA: Every other Saturday. I'd march right up to the desk, over to the Chicago Public Library, the West Side branch, and check out fourteen books.

WALTER: Only fourteen, huh?

ETTA: I was in high school! Fourteen. No questions asked! Dumas, Yerby . . . The esses, I didn't think I was ever going to get through the esses—Shellabarger, Slaughter . . . one a day.

WALTER: At night? How about at night? **(teasing)**

ETTA: At night, I used a flashlight. **(stands up to do a ballet step, twirls around the room)**

WALTER: A flashlight just to read. She's a lucky girl.

ETTA: Lucky? Prepared. Walter, I was prepared. Kept a big one right under my pillow.

WALTER: Lucky you weren't reading what I was reading– **(stands up abruptly, begins to pace)** Philip Roth.

ETTA: Then in college I moved on to Lawrence Durrell, How does he say it—Montolif— James Joyce, You know…experimental, Walter…Oh and Henry Miller…**(rapt)** Henry Miller!

WALTER: I said Philip Roth. Roth's my man.

ETTA: Walter, do you know how bad you look in that Brooks Brothers shirt? Do you? Walter, you're pressed.

WALTER: Come on, Etta. You couldn't read Roth in a day.

ETTA: Now, now let's not jump to conclusions.

WALTER: *Goodbye, Columbus.*

ETTA: Philip Roth . . . I don't particularly care for Philip Roth.

WALTER: **(paces back and forth)** Roth . . . why Roth . . . **(talks over her)** On those long bus trips down South, holding it for hours, 1961, Freedom Rides, no place to stop but long side the road, me and *Goodbye Columbus*. The heat was killing me, rode on that bus so long, I was soaked, me and *Goodbye Columbus*. What's that line? "Blitzkrieg! **(Etta plops down on the sofa.)** Judgment Day! The Lord has lowered his baton." That man could talk to me. One summer night I read that line stretched out on a dirt floor.

ETTA: I'm trying to picture it. **(looks him over)** Walter, stretched out on the floor, all the way down in Mississippi.

WALTER: Last weekend I was playing at the Elks, Monica Stone **("Stone" pronounced as in "stone fox")** came up to me, just wanted to talk. When I told her I was reading Philip Roth, she was speechless, really impressed.

ETTA: **(regular pronunciation)** Monica Stone?

WALTER: Nice and quiet.

ETTA: **(looks straight into his eyes as she talks)** Nice and quiet?

WALTER: That's right. Nice and quiet.

ETTA: Miss Monica Stone. **(imitates Walter's pronunciation, this time only)**

WALTER: She knows how to listen!

ETTA: Oh, but she just wants to talk. Nice and quiet Miss Monica Stone. Well, first of all, I'm not Monica Stone. Monica Stone, my devoted soror, rips the labels out of her own shirts so the pledges can't guess her dirty little secret: they really aren't from Brooks Brothers. Walter… **(eases over)**

WALTER: You and my mother.

ETTA: She's everywhere. This pillow… I love her taste.

WALTER: "Walter, Walter"—you and my mother, you're the only ones ever called me that.

ETTA: And, another thing, the only thing Monica Stone ever used in a library was the telephone...Walter, you've got the longest fingers . . .so long and slender.

WALTER: **(holds his hands out)** Couldn't rough these up...no football

ETTA: For Walter.

WALTER: My mother wouldn't allow it.

ETTA: The better to play Horace Silver with.

WALTER: No rough stuff for the child prodigy. **(his hands are shaking)**

ETTA: Walter Daniels at the piano. Walter, your hands.

WALTER: **(goes over to the window and slams it)** Getting chilly in here. Better pour myself a drink.

ETTA: Will that make them stop shaking?

WALTER: Nothing makes them stop shaking.

ETTA: Let's fix the cushions. There, that's better. **(adjusts a throw pillow and puts her arm around his waist)**

WALTER: **(pulls away)** Nothing.

ETTA: Nothing. Not even a glass of wine? **(goes to cabinet, pours a glass of wine, then hands it to Walter)**

WALTER: **(takes a sip)** Might be coming down with something.

ETTA: Remember when I had the flu? Right there in the infirmary. This girl from the next bed walks right up to me. "What do you think about integration?" Can you believe that? Everywhere I go. That's all they ask me. **(motions to bedroom)** Walter, is that a new bedspread? Walter? I just love your mother's taste.

WALTER: Not one day goes by, not one out of 365. I can see it. Just like yesterday. After we got off the bus, wherever we stayed, I'd never sleep in the bed. Sometimes I'd sit on a sofa, old, beat-up, not like this one. No throw pillows. **(throws pillow on the floor)** You couldn't get me to sleep on a bed, couldn't afford to . . . I'd doze off, every hour or so I'd run to the window, catch a car going by . . . back to the sofa.

ETTA: You were careful, that's all. **(rubs his back)**

WALTER: Careful? Careful? Whatta you know about being careful? You think I was at the Chicago Public Library? I was in Greenwood, Mississippi. And I was scared. Look behind you. Run to the window. Again and again. One night . . . I was staying at this house outside town. A car comes by, stops. You could hear a pin drop. Here comes this loud noise. Me and my boys, we started yelling and screaming. "Move it! Hit the floor!" We knew enough to duck.

ETTA: A bomb?

WALTER: Crash! Right against the side of the garage.

ETTA: Crazy. They're crazy.

WALTER: Few minutes later, we get this call,

ETTA: Your people?

WALTER: **(waves her away)** First just breathing, then this moaning and groaning right in the phone.

ETTA: It was your people. Somebody was hurt?

WALTER: My people? No way! **(beat)** They were hurt alright. **(laughs)** "That's how you'll sound, you dirty SNCC bastard. Next time, nigger, we won't miss." Then they started up again, moaning, "Maybe there won't be enough of you left, nigger... to have any more good times." They were hurt alright. **(laughs)** I could hear 'em in the background. Laughing. Talking about how I oughta start headin' back to the zoo. **(beat)** I didn't mean to get into that . . . all this talking. Don't they teach you how to relax up in Chicago?

(Walter goes over to the record player. He picks an album, Tchaikovsky's *Sleeping Beauty*, and puts it on.)

WALTER: *Sleeping Beauty*.

(He go back to the sofa and sits beside Etta. For a moment, they listen to the music. They move closer to each other. Walter reaches for her hands.)

ETTA: Tchaikovsky . . . I love Tchaikovsky. But you know John Cage . . . John Cage is kind of . . . Walter, you're not going to believe this, but last week I walked up to John Cage after his . . . thing at the auditorium.

(Walter stares off into space. We hear a loud voice from outside the apartment.)

FRANK: Brother Daniels!

(Startled, Walter hurries to the record player to turn it off. In a rush to hide the record, he stumbles and strains his back. Frank, a fraternity brother, enters the room wearing a red and white sweatshirt with a big white K.)

WALTER: **(suddenly jovial and friendly, gives the fraternity handshake)** Brother Smith!

FRANK: Brother Daniels! **(reaches over and tries to look at the record album. Walter puts on a Miles Davis album.)**

WALTER: *Kinda Blue!* — *needs to be funny and cool*

FRANK: Man, you're always into Miles. **(Moving around apartment. Eyes Etta.)** I'm digging your pad, man.

WALTER: This dentist, guy my dad knows, he rents it to me.

FRANK: Mellow, very mellow.

(Frank tries to see album again. Walter moves album away.)

WALTER: Miles, he's my main man— really flips me out. Hey Brother Smith. What's happenin'?

FRANK: Been catching some z's, man.

WALTER: Really.

FRANK: Really. Sheets 101 !

WALTER: **(Walter gestures to Frank with album then finally puts it down.)** Miles! **(They hug each other, laugh, a little physical back and forth.)**

FRANK: **(looking at bookcase, takes out a book)** Yeh, They say Brother Daniels' heavy into the books, philosophizing, deep thinking.

WALTER: Listen to this. **(waves Frank away. Walter up and under counterpoint to Frank.)**

 FRANK: Say he's so heavy when he walks down the street, sidewalk dips and bends. Yeh.

WALTER: You know you just talkin'.

FRANK: Say you so busy booking, you let the party slide right by.

WALTER: Me? **(Walter laughs and rejects idea to Frank's satisfaction.)**

FRANK: That's right. All work. No play. Gotta have time to git down with your boys. Hey man, where you playin' tonight?

WALTER: This little gig ovah to the Elks. Sittin' in with some townies. Git some drums, a horn, heat things up a little. **(sings)** "Cubano-Be, Cubano-Bop." Cracks me up.

FRANK: Incredible, man. Incredible. And speaking of incredible—Etta, how you doin', baby?

ETTA: Just fine.

FRANK: You can say that again. **(The two men laugh. Frank slaps Walter on back. Walter eases away.)**

ETTA: Frank, you are so typical. **(long silence)**

FRANK: You and your nice-lookin' lady plannin' to step out this evening? **(Walter nods. another long silence.)** Ohhh. **(Frank initiates the fraternity handshake.)** Okay, man. Later. **(leaves and closes the door)**

ETTA: Whoa . . . that was a raid. I'm getting the shakes myself.

WALTER: Yeh, that's Frank for you.

(The lights gradually darken.)

ETTA: Right there in the infirmary. This girl in the next bed came up to me. "What do you think about integration?" Can you believe that? Everywhere I go. That's all they ask me. You know, that stuff about Mississippi. When I heard Frank shout like that, my heart . . .

WALTER: What stuff?

ETTA: Stuff. You were talking about how any minute somebody might come up on you—

14

WALTER: Walter's little bedtime story.

ETTA: And it got me thinking about you going down there, that house out in the middle of nowhere, the sound of the crash and how scared…

WALTER: Damn it. Can't you ever stop? I never said anything about being scared.

ETTA: But when I think about how it…all that crazy… groaning and moaning. **(Walter grabs her.)** Maybe we wouldn't be here like this.

WALTER: **(laughs)** Like what? Look, I told you before.

ETTA: What if something had happened, what if we'd never met?

prolepsic?

WALTER: Look at you. Ready to cry. Is that all you ever think about? Look at me. Walter Daniels. You think I go to bed, get up thinking about some cracker trying to blow me away? Stuff happens all the time. If something happens, it won't be to me. **(Begins to pace back and forth across the room. Walks as if his back is bothering him.)**

ETTA: Walter?

WALTER: Waiting around so I can turn the other cheek. Standing back, holding on. Rule One. Under no circumstances are you to fight back. Under no circumstances are you to defend yourself. Goodbye, Columbus! **(saracastically)** Go on over to the Elks. Frank's ready to party.

(Etta protests.)

ETTA: Walter, maybe after you come back, we can go over to campus, grab some food.

WALTER: **(turns away)** You're still talking.

ETTA: I could meet you at the Elks. Top floor. Right? It's like a concert. I'm into concerts, Walter. Really, I am.

WALTER: Concert? I'm playing at the Elks, Etta. That's all. I am not giving a concert. Not tonight, okay?

ETTA: Let's get all dressed up. Make an appearance. You know. Clothes. Pile it all on. I'll wear jewelry. Lots and lots of jewelry. Piles and piles of stuff. Walter? Then I make my entrance. I'm at this concert, Walter. Picture it.

WALTER: **(turns away)** Etta, you're still talking.

ETTA: This…musician…John Cage...the man actually asked me, he wanted to know where I bought my necklace. He walked right up to me. Just like this, said: 'Try it on me, kid.' So I slip it around his neck. Walter, like this. He was stunned. Said 'How much you want for that necklace?' So I said to him… Watch me, Walter. Watch me. I'm wearing this really incredible coat I bought at the Junior League. Everybody's dressed up. We're all crammed in there together in this big round house with a ceiling this high. Round House! It's a happening. Everybody's trying to out dress everybody else. Just to impress John Cage. But John Cage really doesn't care about any of it. He just doesn't care. He's blowing his nose in this Kleenex. Then he's rubbing the Kleenex against the microphone. Takes out this comb. Bangs on the mike. Makes all these crazy sounds. You have to understand the situation, Walter. So I say to John Cage "It's not for sale." Can you believe that?

WALTER: **(moves away)** I'm getting stiff.

ETTA: Call the Elks. Say your fever's out of control. We could stay here and study—catch up on things. **(moves closer. Walter moves away.)** Walter, when you get back tonight, I'll still be here, I won't leave.

WALTER: Not tonight, okay? It's my back…I'm trying to understand this. I'm trying to have a conversation with you. I'm trying to talk!

ETTA: That bottle of wine over there. We'll finish it off. I'll show you my new City Lights — Allen Ginsberg, Lawrence Ferlinghetti— It goes like this, Walter:

They
are silent together
as in a flowered field upon the summer couch which must
be hers
And he holds her still
so passionately
holds her head to his
so gently so insistently
to make her turn her lips to his

(very long pause)

WALTER: So you really don't like Philip Roth?

(Etta lies down on sofa and Walter sits erect, at attention beside her. Lights fade to dark.)

ACT ONE SCENE TWO

(Music up. Miles Davis, *Kind of Blue*. A moment of transition. Music Fades. Walter and Etta are walking outside. They have left his apartment.)

ETTA: When I told them I was from the West Side they expected me to be different, you know, lowdown, gut bucket, rough and tumble. I was actually just the opposite. Green, Walter. Green. Green. Green. All I knew was the FM station. The day I arrived in Champaign Urbana I was a virgin **(long pause)** musically.

WALTER: Okay. That's a new one. She was musically pure.

ETTA: Pure as the driven snow. At night, in high school, I'd listened to Brahms and Beethoven and Bach. When I got here, even the student station wasn't much better, they were always playing Haydn.

WALTER: And Tchaikovsky.

ETTA: Tchaikovsky…sometimes…Then I went to this John Cage concert!!! Zowie!

WALTER: Pretty proud of yourself, huh?

ETTA: Remember? That concert I told you about? Remember? You know. John Cage?

WALTER: The one where you wore that coat from the Junior League and that necklace, some big dangling thing around your neck. Don't know a thing about him.

(They stop for a minute.)

ETTA: You were probably out South, going to the Sutherland.

WALTER: Once in awhile.

ETTA: Listening to Monk and Miles.

WALTER: After school? I was practicing the piano. Before that, I was taking as long as I could to get home.

ETTA: House after house after house. All these houses. They all look the same. Some day I'm gonna live in a big round house with a ceiling this high. I'll listen to all the music in the universe. **(looks in the other direction)** Hey, wait a minute, I thought we were going to the Elks.

WALTER: You walk to get where you're going. Sometimes you stop. Check things out.

ETTA: Stop!

WALTER: South Side West Side. 63rd and Cottage. 16th and Hamlin. It's all the same.

ETTA: **(louder)** Stop! **(They pause.)** I said I thought we were going to the Elks.

WALTER: Where'd you hear that?

ETTA: Don't play games with me. Back at your place. You told Frank…

WALTER: I told Frank I was going to the Elks. I'm walking you home.

ETTA: Walter, Walter, always in charge, aren't you? At first I thought you were lost or something. Not Walter.

WALTER: Did you ever walk past rows and rows of neat little houses, all lined up? City houses. On the way home from school, I'd walk past the projects, through the alley past the chicken shack at 63rd and Cottage. Run in for a sack of French fries, throw on a little a Miss Mary's homemade ketchup. Kick a pop bottle, real hard, the way the light hits it, you could swear it was worth something, a piece of broken glass, shining like a ring . **(takes Etta's hand. Holds it up to the light)** Did I ever tell you about this brother, knew him since grade school? Went to the same high school too. I was 12, skinny little kid, already in the ninth grade. Larry was old, 15 or 16. Same grade. Larry. He was always fooling around.Wouldn't do a thing the teacher said. That same year Larry had an accident, playing with this bottle of strong stuff, from chemistry class. Mixing and pouring. Fooling around. The bottle, the whole thing, blew up right in his face. Larry. **(pulling)**The brother didn't even know enough to duck. I was sitting right next to him, didn't get a scratch. **(yells)** He kept screaming and screaming. I moved close to him. Like this. Waved my hands across Larry's face. He couldn't see a thing. **(beat)** Everybody else was yelling too, crying and hugging on Larry. The teacher rushed Larry out of the room. Next thing I knew he was going to this school for the blind. Overnight. That's when Larry learned how to listen. Didn't have his eyes, so everything else was double sharp. The brother could hear everything. Couldn't see but he could hear the least little sound.

Every day, after school, I'd wait till they let Larry off the bus, then I'd walk him home. Every day. Me and Larry. We'd walk a little. Then stop and talk. **(long pause)** Got to know each other, better and better…in ways, so many ways… Sometimes we'd get lost on purpose. It's funny. Still can't believe it myself. It's like he has eyes in the back of his head, but I know he can't see. Every time I go home. I go see Larry. Wants to know where I've been. Lately. I can't get by old Larry. If I leave something out. He catches me. Larry can't see but he knows exactly where I've been and where I'm going.

ETTA: Larry, he knows about Greenwood, about you in the house, about the phone calls?

WALTER: All of it. He knows about it all.

(Etta backs away then walks back to Walter. After they pause for a moment, Etta pecks Walter on the cheek. She enters a room at the sorority house.)

ACT ONE SCENE THREE

(The Pi Lambda house. The pledges are hanging out upstairs in a large room on the top floor of the sorority house that serves as living quarters for Etta and her sister pledges. "Chances Are" by Johnny Mathis is playing on the record player.)

(Etta waltzes into the room. Dominates the space.)

SHIRLEY: **(Shirley is on the phone. Yells out.)** Look at her. Getting happy! **(beat)** Hello.

ETTA: Hey, Shirley.

SHIRLEY: Grinning like Christmas day.

ETTA: **(to Monica.)** Soror Monica.

MONICA: Uuummm.

SHIRLEY: Look at Etta. She's been to church.

(Etta waltzes behind a screen. Throws her shoes out one by one.)

MONICA: **(throws shoes across the room)** Who does she think she is?

(Etta comes out wearing a pair of black pants)

ETTA: Etta Bradshaw, the first Black . . .

MONICA: **(She is aware she is pretty, wears a short haircut.)** The first Negro.

ETTA: The first black native of Delphi, Tennessee . . .

MONICA: We've heard this before.

ETTA: **(clears her throat)** Etta--The first Black native of Delphi, Tennessee to resist repeated offers of full tuition to Tennessee A & I and Fisk, pleas made by various aunts, uncles, and utterly caring relatives and, instead, to courageously attend a major Northern university with a notoriously high flunkout rate.

SHIRLEY: Another first.

ETTA: She leaves Delphi, Tennessee for the Great West Side of Chicago.
MONICA: Slum...

SHIRLEY: Never been on the West Side. Drove through it but I never stopped.

MONICA:. Country folks moving up to the big city. Got a train ticket and a suitcase. Packing up and heading for the West Side. My mama told me, if you ever get lost over there, don't get outta your car and don't walk around .

ETTA: **(to Shirley)** Miss South Side. Monica Stone. She's Stone South Side.
Thinks she knows all about the West Side. The West Side is everybody and everything, out of work to rolling in dough, all crammed in to a bunch of city blocks. (to Monica) Trust me. You don't know a thing.

MONICA: I know everything I need to know about broken down, run down, double parked cars on little bitty streets. Shabby looking....

FEEZIE: **(wakes up. scratches hair, which sticks straight up.)** Leave Etta alone.

SHIRLEY: Feezie.   The sleeping giant comes to life.

(Monica puts on "What'd I Say" by Ray Charles on record player. Sings the first bar to Etta.)

MONICA: "Tell your mama, tell your pa/Gonna send you back to Arkansas...All right, hey, hey, tell me, what I say? Da-dada-da-da, Tell me, What I say..."

ETTA: Pledge Monica Stone, The first colored--oops, Negro--to select a record... **(Monica and Etta face each other, break out in a dance, The Slop, eye each other, then stop.)**

SOROR BANKS: **(offstage on intercom)** Quiet up there. **(beat)** Surprise. Surprise. Lambda pledge class, we've got company. **(excited noise)**

 SHIRLEY: Surprise. Surprise.

ETTA: Shhh...Soror Banks. **(Record up and under. Fades out. Laughter)** Big, strong Lambda line. **(Feezie, Monica and Shirley stand behind Etta.)**

SOROR BANKS: **(on intercom)** I said keep it down. We're about to make history. That's right, ladies. History. In case you haven't heard, we've been chosen by the DC office, given the special honor of hosting a visit by our National president. Our national president, who just happens to be standing right next to me with your Dean of Women, Dean Hortense Drummond.

(Noise, moving around chairs, etc.)

ETTA: Now she tells me. "In case you haven't heard!"

MONICA: **(to Etta)** Newsflash! In case you haven't heard, actives don't tell their business to a pledge till they're good and ready.

SOROR BANKS: **(on intercom)**: If you're good you can come down . . . shortly.

MONICA: **(to Etta)** They're not calling you down, anyway.

SHIRLEY: OOOH.

ETTA: Says who? **(Etta is still dancing to "What'd I Say.")**

MONICA: Look at her... West Side...

ETTA: Great West Side!

MONICA: A ghetto queen talk to the National President? Better not go out South.

ETTA: Says who?

MONICA: Says me, Monica Stone. You? Talk to the National President? You've got so many demerits they wouldn't let you say hello to Godzilla.

ETTA: That's cause they keep him on the South Side, up the street from your house. Little man, say hi to Monica. Come on, little fellow, pretty please?

(Everybody laughs. Etta starts dancing around again.)

SHIRLEY: Okay. Okay. Let's have it.

ETTA: Been hittin' the books, Shirley. Ready to relax. Go to some clubs. You know. The Sutherland.

MONICA: You?

ETTA: Out South.

MONICA: Down South.

(Monica Stone goes back to "What'd I Say" by Ray Charles on record player. Dances around. Gets in Etta's face. Feezie comes alive. Women start dancing together. Loud laughter in background. Feezie slumps down to go back to sleep. Shirley pulls her up.)

SHIRLEY: Feezie, Miss Frezia Amalita Jones. Voice major. She slept so long, her hair's dented. Send this poor child downstairs to sing for the President.

MONICA: Go on down there, Feezie, Sing the Pi Lambda song for Soror Banks. Keep us out of trouble.

SOROR BANKS: (**offstage**) All pledges observe mandatory dress code until further notice. Absolutely, no pants. Please.

MONICA: You heard her, Etta. They don't wanna see your behind downstairs.

FEEZIE: Leave Etta alone. She's got big plans, ideas, so many it would make your head swim.

(Etta waltzes around. Shirley notices.)

ETTA: Plans, Shirley, plans….

SHIRLEY: Hmmmm.

MONICA: **(grabs magazine from underneath Feezie)**
Eeekkk, she fell asleep on my *Ebony.*

ETTA: Her Ebony **(Picks up *Ebony*. Directs comment to
Monica.)** She's reading "Ten Ways to Trap a Man."
(Shirley grabs magazine.)

FEEZIE: Firsts of The First, the first Negro jet pilot from
Oklahoma. Oooh. **(they gather around the magazine)**

SHIRLEY**: (grabs magazine)** Date with a Dish. Black
eyed peas and salmon croquettes.

 FEEZIE: Hey, wait a minute, **(grabs magazine)** A new
chapter of the Links…cotillions, cotillions, cotillions.

(Music fades)

ETTA: A few days before I applied for college my mother
and I engaged in a deep, dark conversation about why I
wasn't going to either Tennessee A & I or Fisk.

MONICA: You heard her. You heard her. Her mama was
tryin to tell her something. Buy this child a ticket. Send her
down South.

ETTA: She was worried about my opportunities. Clubs,
parties, cotillions the kind with black bow ties and pink,
frothy, net off- the- shoulder numbers.

FEEZIE: If you're from the West Side, you have to try harder. Way harder.

ETTA: There was this cotillion she kept talking about, one where everybody wore white gloves.

(Etta plops down on bed.)

FEEZIE: Come on, Etta, we can't go down there without you.

ETTA: Maybe you ought to get used to the idea. The idea of being free. Free, Feezie, free as the breeze.

alliteration! / onomatopeoia

FEEZIE: Come on, let's go downstairs.

ETTA: You see these pants?

MONICA: Uh-huh.

ETTA: They express my original dark-skinned self.

MONICA: Talkin' pants.

ETTA: They never let me down, any color, they go with anything: red, blue, green, sweaters, shirts, after five, anytime.

MONICA: It's a good thing they gave her a behind. **(to Etta)** If you didn't have a behind, you'd be wasted. **(Etta throws pillow.)**

(Etta dials the phone and waltzes around hugging the phone.)

SHIRLEY: I bet I know who she's trying to call.

MONICA: Godzilla.

ETTA: He doesn't take calls.

MONICA: He would from you.

ETTA: The regional award for Miss Superficiality goes to
. . . **(Yells to Monica Stone as she's leaving)** March 7,
1963---News flash. Freedom Riders board the bus! <u>Down
South.</u> But Pledge Monica Stone still feels the need to
reflect on the size of my behind.

MONICA: **(yells out as she is leaving)** Listen to her. How
many demerits did they give her for wearing pants on
campus? **(Monica exits room.)**

SHIRLEY: **(to Monica)** Five.

ETTA: This place is driving me crazy.

SHIRLEY: You ought to be used to that.

ETTA:. Why is it that this world is full of so many
prehistoric people who just can't see the writing on the
wall? This is 1963! No time for the ordinary.

(Monica comes back.)

MONICA: **(breathlessly)** Guess who I just saw
downstairs?

ETTA: The national president.

MONICA: She was wearing this navy and white Chanel
suit with pearls, seams this straight . . . And she was in the

Marines with Dean Drummond. That's why she's here. They're having a reunion and you can't go down because you're wearing pants.

(Etta is rummaging through her dresser.)

SHIRLEY: Etta's a beatnik….sometimes.

FEEZIE: I saw her one day. Wearing this pair of black pants on campus.

MONICA: Her?

FEEZIE: Her? I know what beatniks wear. All black. Black pants, black top, black shoes…black.

(overlapping)

SHIRLEY: She's. She's…

FEEZIE: …deep.

SHIRLEY: She likes weird—

FEEZIE: Heavy. She's heavy.

SHIRLEY: **(corrects herself)** unusual things….stuff you've never heard of . Don't you, Etta?

ETTA: **(to Monica)** At times, I choose to wear black. Other times I choose the Elle look as in Elle magazine, or the sorority look as in matching sweater sets. They all have their validity. I wouldn't be caught dead without my sweater sets.

(Monica bends over Etta as Etta looks through her clothes. Etta picks up Brooks Brothers shirt and puts it on.)

MONICA: News flash: Behold the well-dressed beatnik. A Bernard Altman bernamere sweater set and matching skirt. A black sheath dress. **(checks out Etta's shirt)** Wait a minute, oh my God, she's wearing my Brooks Brothers shirt.

ETTA: Uh, uh. Here. Here's yours. **(Etta goes to Monica's dresser and grabs one of her shirts.)** You can tell. See. It walks like a Brooks Brothers shirt and it talks like a Brooks Brothers Shirt. Wait a minute. No label. **(Etta holds up shirt.)** She buys hers at Sears and rips out the label so Walter Daniels just *might* think they're from Brooks Brothers.

SHIRLEY: Really?

ETTA: That's right, Walter Daniels. Walter's pressed. He walked me home. **(to Monica)** Really. Tonight. Tonight, Walter's playing at the Elks. He begged me and begged me to go with him. Had to let him down. Maybe I'll give him a call.

MONICA: Walter Daniels? And you? **(laughs loudly)** Walter Daniels? Don't make me laugh. **(Fusses with chair.)**

ETTA: We stopped by his place, relaxed a little, then he walked me home.

MONICA: From the train station.

(Shirley and Feezie laugh.)

SOROR BANKS: Quiet up there.We want you dressed and downstairs in 5 minutes. No tennis shoes, please.

MONICA: **(to Etta)** You? Splib!

MONICA: Walter? Uhuh. I bet it was a white boy. You know you like greys.

ETTA: Look at you, grey yourself.

MONICA: I saw you on campus talking to those white boys.

ETTA: Now I know why she can't pass P.E. Too busy following me around.

MONICA: I saw you at the Music Building Friday night, partyin' with all those greys. Acting white.

ETTA: I was on official business.

MONICA: So was I.

ETTA: Following me around. **(beat)** Spy!

MONICA: In the streets.

ETTA: Spy!

MONICA: Listening to gutbucket. **(Pushes Etta.)**

ETTA: Muddy Waters is not white. **(Pushes Monica back.)**

(Shoving match between Monica and Etta. Feezie rushes up and pushes her way between them.)

FEEZIE: Leave Etta alone. She can't help being from the West Side.

ETTA: **(to Feezie)** The great West Side. Please! (**to Monica)** Friday night I was at a meeting of The Campus Blues Society. I can't help it if everybody there's white. I'm studying music.

FEEZIE: Hadn't heard that before.

ETTA: The music of the universe, Feezie. It's big. Huge. You think I can study one or two people? A bunch of white guys from the 18th century? I have to study it all.

MONICA: She's studying white folks.

FEEZIE: More and more white folks.

ETTA: I'm studying the blues.

SHIRLEY: And the labels on Walter Daniels's shirts.

ETTA: History, Shirley. The history of Muddy Waters.

MONICA: OOOh, she listens to that stuff?

ETTA: And Howlin' Wolf.

SHIRLEY: **(to Etta)** Better not tell your mother. She'd have a fit.

FEEZIE: That's right. Etta's mother is the mother of the church, and you know they don't want to hear all that.

FEEZIE: Pi Lambda women don't do that stuff.

ETTA: What stuff?

FEEZIE: You know.

MONICA: Stuff.

SHIRLEY: Pi Lambda women. In by ten.

FEEZIE: Men! Out the front door.

MONICA: **(to Etta)** I oughta call her right now. This child needs to go to church. **(goes over and stands by the phone)**

ETTA: Put that phone down.

(Monica laughs)

MONICA: I've been getting a whole lot of phone calls myself. From Walter Daniels…Walter. That's right. He wants to take me to the Sutherland to see Miles.

ETTA: You and Walter? What would he want with you?

MONICA: He said I was just what he was looking for--- a certain kind of lady, refined, sophisticated…

ETTA: …and superficial! Walter? Walter's into politics and SNCC and things like that.

MONICA: OOOh, SNCC.

ETTA: Walter Daniels is a very deep thinker. He happens to be in that Student Non-Violent Coordinating Committee.

MONICA: OOOh. A coordinator. Bigtime! Then what would he want with you? **(goes over and fidgets with the phone)** Me and Walter. We've been to the Sutherland. Two or three times. I was wearing this black sheath dress. Fitted. Little pumps. Walter was fine. Pressed. Said he wouldn't be caught dead with something like you---from the West Side.

ETTA: Come over here and say that again.

MONICA: Ghetto.

(Etta grabs a chair and throws it at Monica. Monica screams a blood-curdling scream and ducks.)

MONICA: That's it. That's it. I'm telling the actives She threw it at me. She threw the chair at me. You make...**(lunges at Etta. Shirley holds on to Monica. Stops her from leaving.)**

ETTA: ..ME SICK. You and this whole place.

SOROR BANKS: **(offstage)** Pi Lambda pledges, beginning immediately, you're all grounded.   I want a full report on this!

MONICA: She hit me with that chair.

(Monica storms out of the room. She's almost out the door. Shirley grabs her.)

SHIRLEY: Don't you say a word to Soror Banks. You hear? **(Monica pushes Shirley out of the way and storms**

out. (to the group) Better get some sleep. There'll be duckwalking tonight.

SOROR BANKS: **(offstage)** Be prepared to recite the entire in depth history of Pi Lambda. 1900 to the present!

FEEZIE: Sing and squat. sing and squat. I'm not singing ABC's at 3 am, not tonight. Alpha, Beta, Gamma, Delta...

SHIRLEY: Git on board, Feezie. Soror Banks crossed the burning sands. We gotta cross 'em too.

ETTA: Shirley . . . I can't stand being fenced in. If I don't feel like wearing chartreuse and white every Friday, just because I'm pledging Pi Lambda, so what???

SHIRLEY: So what? So, we're all you got, whether you like it or not.

SOROR BANKS: **(offstage)** Remember ladies, stockings and pumps on the main floor. Dean Drummond has consented to join her comrade in arms, our national president, for this evening's meal. **(pause)** Pot roast!

(Etta slips over to the door.)

ETTA: I think I'll go meet the National President..

(Etta runs out. Shirley and Feezie grab at her on her way out. She slips by them.)

ETTA: **(turns as she exits)** and say hi to Dean Drummond.

FEEZIE: Etta! **(Etta runs out.)**

SOROR BANKS: **(offstage)** Pledge attire ignored. Pi Lambda rules broken and abandoned. Pledge Etta Bradshaw grounded until further notice.

(Etta bursts into the room. Throws open the closet door, grabs a suitcase and throws it on her bed.)

ETTA: I'm moving out.

FEEZIE: **(crying pleadingly)** Etta, we can't go over without you.

SHIRLEY: **(to Etta)** Look at Feezie. Look what you started. Alright, Miss lady, you'll end up back in the dorms.

ETTA: **(rushes back in. reaches for another suitcase)** No, I won't.

SHIRLEY: Oh, you won't?

(Etta continues to pack.)

SHIRLEY: Okay! I've got it! You're planning to shack up with the three bears.

ETTA: I'm looking at rooms off campus.

SHIRLEY: Off campus??? You'll never find a room.

ETTA: I won't? **(Feezie covers her mouth.)** Shirley, don't worry, it'll be fine. **(laughing)**

SHIRLEY: I can see the posters: "What would you do if colored moved into your neighborhood? Meeting tonight at 8 in the school gym."

FEEZIE: This is too much trouble. I'm gonna start sleeping, sleep more and more and . . . sleep for the rest of the semester.

ETTA: **(to Feezie)** Free, Feezie.

FEEZIE: I don't want to be free. At least not right now. Mama was right. About bein free and all that stuff. She said "Feezie, hold off on the high jinks." In by ten! All I wanna do is order out.

SHIRLEY: Feezie, I thought voice majors were on a special diet, bird food or some such thing.

FEEZIE: Po Boy's good for birds. **(beat)** I'm too sad to sing . . . Frezia Amalita Jones is too sad to sing. If I wanted to be free . . . I never woulda moved in here in the first place.

(Etta alone on the stage, looks around the room. picks up things. dials phone.)

MOTHER: Hello.

ETTA: Mama.

MOTHER: Uumhuh.

ETTA: It's Etta.

MOTHER: You know I know who you are. My little Pi Lammy Lammy…

ETTA: Ah, Mama.

MOTHER: I've been telling all my gal pals about you. "I'll be down there initiation night, going to see my Etta, my little Pi Lammy Lammy Soror."

ETTA: Mama…

MOTHER: Uuuum

ETTA: Mama, I'm…

MOTHER: Ooom Huh. I'm getting my things together right now. Found the prettiest dress made out of that whipped cream. That's all they're wearing these days. Perfect for the train. Won't wrinkle at all.

ETTA: Mama, I've decided not to pledge.

(Silence.)

ETTA: Mama? Are you still there?

MOTHER: I'm here.

ETTA: Can you hear me? I said I've decided not to pledge.

MOTHER: I heard you. Etta, have you lost every ounce of sense you were born with. Have you? Baby, do you know what you're giving up?

(Etta moans.)

MOTHER: This is about the rest of your life. The rest of your life, honey. **(beat)** Aah! You got in some kind of argument. I know you. Had to have things your way and only your way. But you'll go back. You will, won't you? **(long pause)** You'll say you were in a bad mood or something. Lost control. Didn't mean any of it. Not one word. You calmed down, smoothed out all those ruffled feathers, cool as a cucumber and you're back on board.

ETTA: Mama…I can't!

MOTHER: I'll come down there right now. We'll straighten it out.

ETTA: Uuu-uh.

MOTHER: I'll call the home office. That's what I'll do. What was her name? Soror….

ETTA: No, Mama. I can't. I just can't.

MOTHER: You're ruining your whole life. Do you hear me?

ETTA: Yes ma'am.

MOTHER: You do?

ETTA: Mama. I'm sorry. I know how it is when you've got everything all laid out. Planned. You're big on your plans. I bet you've been getting ready for this for days.

MOTHER: Days? Years, Etta. Years.

ETTA: Mama, I just can't. I'm sorry. I know how is. A Pi Lambda legacy, just like you and Aunt Mildred. **(sighs into phone)** I'm moving out of the house. And changing my major.

MOTHER: I was just getting ready for my bath. I think I'll go take a nice hot bath. Put in some of that scented oil you gave me for Christmas.

ETTA: I'm changing my major to Music History

MOTHER: **(frazzled)** Music what?

ETTA: Music History.

MOTHER: Music History? Playing what, where? Is it listening to LP's??? What kind of job is that?

ETTA: But Mama, you love music. *Rhapsody in Blue.* You'll go anywhere, pay anything to hear it. Every time it's on Ed Sullivan, I can hear you crying.

(Mother sobs.)

MOTHER: Look Etta, I can give you my copy of *Rhapsody in Blue.* You can play it all day long. **(click)**

(Lights up. Etta, upset after the phone call, is throwing things in her suitcase.)

FEEZIE: **(wails)** Etta's packing her things.

ETTA: **(to Shirley)** That was my mother. Shirley, I've never seen her like this. She was beside herself. Said this was my chance to make something of myself. She says if I leave the house, I'll ruin my life, maybe even end up in jail.

SHIRLEY: If I told my mother I was leaving the house…

ETTA: **(timidly)** Then I mentioned I was not going to major in elementary ed….

SHIRLEY: . . . and changed my major from Accounting to Music History. She'd come down here…

FEEZIE: Etta's majoring in the music of the universe.

SHIRLEY: The universe. Yeh, She'd send me to another universe and spend my tuition on a vacation to Hawaii.

ETTA: Feezie, you're a music major.

SHIRLEY: She sings.

FEEZIE: …music.

ETTA: Okay. Music. I thought if I mentioned *Rhapsody in Blue*. **(cries out)** Mama! She calls it her theme song. I thought she'd understand.

SHIRLEY: Understand? Understand her only child leaving the sorority two weeks before initiation? A mother's dream? And a legacy to boot?

(Sits back down with group. The room is darker.)

FEEZIE: **(crying)** Getting ready to cross those burnin' sands. All this time we're side by side. Me and my sands, Shirley, Monica. …**(looks at Etta)**

ETTA: You'll get along without me.

FEEZIE: **(cries)** Etta, you're the captain of the ship.

(Etta comforts Feezie.)

42

ETTA: Captain of the Ship? Feezie, what they saw in me I'll never know. I've never led anything in my whole life. I was on the ship, but I sure wasn't the captain.

FEEZIE: Etta's heavy. She's got big plans, ideas. and they don't include me.

(Shirley rummages through papers on her desk. whispers to Feezie. hands her a newspaper.)

FEEZIE: The best grades in the house. My sand. Gone. I'll be up in the middle of the night singing all by myself...

ETTA: It's like an audition, Feezie. You know about auditions. You just stand up and sing.

SHIRLEY: I'm gonna lay it all out. Nice and clear. You're almost a junior in college. You've paid all your initiation fees. Plus you don't have anywhere else to go. Listen to this ad. "Room, pleasant, convenient to campus. **(emphasis)** Whites only." Tell Etta about auditions, Feezie. Etta...listen...please.

FEEZIE: My cousin Lula got bombed out back home, bought this house in Trumbull Park. Zoweee! Phizzzz . . . All she had left was a set of cup towels and her station wagon. They probably won't bother you that much, you're not buying a house, just livin' in a little old room.

SHIRLEY: You've got two choices. Live in the dorms or stay here with us.

ETTA: Walter Daniels...

SHIRLEY: ...Walter Daniels is a grad student. They're not gonna let you live off campus.

(Etta starts packing again.)

SHIRLEY: You can leave all your sweater sets here, just in case.

FEEZIE: She can take the ones with the monograms

MONICA: **(reenters, shaking fist at Etta)** Do you know what I've been doing? I've been down there talking to actives. Trying to get you off the hook. They've got a list this long on Etta Bradshaw. Breaking every rule in the book. Wearin' pants on the ground floor! **(to rest of group)** I was down there trying to make excuses for her.

FEEZIE: Etta's leaving.

MONICA: Gutbucket.

SHIRLEY: You hear that, Monica? Our sand's movin' out of the house.

MONICA: Leaving?

SHIRLEY: Leaving Pi Lambda.

MONICA: Leaving where? Nobody wants her.

(Etta continues packing.)

ETTA: We'll see about that.

MONICA: Ghetto queen. Now I know she's from the West Side. Ghetto queen. She almost killed me with that chair.

FEEZIE: Ettaaaaa !!This is breaking my heart. When I get like this, it does something to my vocal chords. See? **(clutches throat)** Feezie, Feezie, control. Girl, you can do it.

MONICA: Look at you. You're living at the Pi Lambda house. White girls in Chi O don't have to do half the stuff we do. That's right. We make it hard 'cause we got it hard. **(to Feezie)** You're not the first and you won't be the last.

ETTA: Feezie, plenty of people live off campus. **(to Shirley)** Walter Daniels has his own place…fixed up and everything…

MONICA: Hah!

SHIRLEY: … Yeh and how did he get it? Walter Daniels has connections. His pappy's a dentist.

MONICA: And his mama runs the Links…outta your league.

SHIRLEY: He's got friends in high places.

ETTA:Shirley? You with me on this? **(Shirley reaches out for her Etta's hand.)**

SHIRLEY: You know what they say? A hard head...

MONICA: Makes a soft behind.

ETTA: **(to Monica)** Look, all I'm trying to do is move out!

FEEZIE: If this keeps up, I'll have to cancel Spring Recital.

45

MONICA: So you're leaving? **(sees Etta packing her things)**

ETTA: **(to Monica)** You heard me. I'm through.

MONICA: Through? **(Etta turns away, preoccupied)** You think you can just walk out that door. Like a white girl in a bad mood. This is for real. If you leave now, there's no turning back.

(Etta is looking around the room for her things.)

Hey, hey **(yells)** WHAT'D I SAY? Over here. I'm talking to you. I was downstairs. Bustin' my butt for you. Beggin Soror Banks. Just give her another chance. Please just one more chance. You think you can pick up and leave, don't you? Guess what? Right now. It's the right time. Our time. Look at you. Miss Thing. You wanna act the way they do. Call a cab. Walk out. Likety Split. Uh-uh. We don't do that. You see this little pin? You've got one too. A pledge pin. Well, I'm getting ready to trade mine in---for something big. Sit downstairs with the actives. Big as I wanna be. When I get up in the morning. I'll look all around. Take it all in. **(picks up a few things)** This house. This is ours. Ours. All of it.

My whole family came up through Pi Lambda. My mother. And my mother's mother. All sorors. Sorors. That's right. Pi Lambda is everything to me. My heart, my soul. You can't leave now. We're gettin ready to cross the burnin' sands. Do you know who you are? Look at you. You're the captain of the ship. You're locked into this.

(Monica goes over to her bed and sits quietly. Lights down.)

ACT ONE SCENE FOUR

(The next day: Music up. Miles Davis. Etta is looking for rooms with Shirley and Feezie. Shirley holds the newspaper. Business like and organized, she is checking things off. Keeping things straight.)

SHIRLEY: **(wearily)** Okay. The top of the list: "Roomer, to rent quiet room over modest establishment, must be clean and neat, no colored applicants appreciated."

FEEZIE: Etta's a test case.

SHIRLEY: She's a case alright.

ETTA: Let's call it something like reverse snobbery. I'm only interested in going where I'm not wanted. Silly me. **(They open the door. It creaks. They go in.)** Cool. Things are pretty quiet, huh?

FEEZIE: Funeral parlors are always pretty quiet unless there's a wake or something.

SHIRLEY: Why am I doing this? I coulda stayed at the house. Studied from my accounting exam or my econ exam **(shouts at Etta)** or my psychiatric exam. I've got two hour exams tomorrow and I've got time to go on a wild goose chase. Shirley, Shirley, Shirley. Coulda stayed at the house. Had left over pot roast and potato salad. No. No. Not me. That's too much like right.

ETTA: Hello. Hello out there!

(no answer)

VOICE: Hello. Hello.

(no answer)

(Door opens slightly. Suddenly, a woman appears in shadows, looks at them)

ETTA: Hello.

(Woman screams. They scream back.)

WOMAN: Out, out, get out, damn you! Or I'll call the cops!

(They rush out.)

FEEZIE: **(Feezie holds newspaper.)** Next stop!

SHIRLEY: **(looks at Etta)** You're sure you called first?

ETTA: Relax, Shirley. It's fine. I was approved by phone interview. Mrs. Hurley's rooming house is one of two houses on campus that without a doubt are approved for undergrad women.

SHIRLEY: **(reads newspaper slowly)** Undergrad women, okay? Undergrad women, **(keeps reading)** are we leaving out something here?

FEEZIE: **(reads newspaper ad)** A charming little place with spacious community bath room …

ETTA: And no privacy. You can hear the toilet flush at 3 am.

48

SHIRLEY: (**moans**) Whose idea was this anyway? (**to Etta**) Girl, you don't know when to stop.

ETTA: Here we are! Mrs. Hurley's!

(**Shirley, Etta, and Feezie approach cautiously. They knock on door. Then knock again. Woman opens door. Mrs. Hurley is in the shadows. Conversation takes place in the doorway or on the side of the stage.**)

MRS. HURLEY: Hello?

ETTA: Mrs. Hurley? I'm Etta. You talked to me over the phone.

MRS. HURLEY: Oh my.

ETTA: Remember?

MRS. HURLEY: Oh my....(**fanning herself**) This weather. Wouldn't know it was May would you? Running every one of my fans. Don't mind the light bill. Not a bit! It's getting hotter and hotter... What are you?

ETTA: Ma'am?

MRS. HURLEY: Are you Indian from India?

ETTA: No ma'am.

MRS. HURLEY: Are you foreign?

ETTA: No ma'am.

MRS. HURLEY: What are you, then?

ETTA: I'm colored.

MRS. HURLEY: Oh, my God.(**starts to shake more, very upset, crying**) I don't know, I don't know. . . . Do you go to a colored school?

MRS. HURLEY: (**to Shirley**) Are all your teachers colored? Are these your teachers?

SHIRLEY: No ma'am.

ETTA: (**Mrs. Hurley keeps saying "I don't know" up and under.**) But I thought I'd need some help to take my things upstairs. My friends Shirley and Feezie, they came along to help.

MRS. HURLEY: (**to Etta**) Are those farm pants you're wearing? Do you work on a farm? (**Keeps saying "Oh my God." Up and Under**)

(**Mrs. Hurley is freaking out. All three of them are at the door by now.**)

MRS. HURLEY: I've only got one room.

ETTA: Don't worry ma'am, they won't stay overnight.

(**Mrs. Hurley looks them over. Blocks the door.**)

MRS. HURLEY: (**screams**) No. Noooo. Noooooooo.

(**Slams the door on them. Etta, Shirley and Feezie leave. Lights down.**)

END OF ACT ONE

ACT TWO

SCENE ONE

(Walter is in his apartment. He's talking to his father on the phone. He stands next to a table stacked with papers. Wears sleeveless undershirt and pajama bottoms.)

FATHER: Tell me about school.

WALTER: My thesis?

FATHER: I want to hear all about it.

WALTER: A lot of paperwork. Dad. Whew! Mountains and mountains of stuff. I'm trying to wind things up...

FATHER: ...Trying to?

WALTER: ...For sure, Dad. Definitely. By the end of the spring...

FATHER: Alright, alright

WALTER: I'll finish it...I will...

FATHER: ...with all you've been doing?

WALTER: I'll get it done, Dad. I'll be home before you know it. You can count on that. (beat) I'd better talk to Mama.

FATHER: Hmmph. The woman's preparing for battle.

WALTER: …her cotillion…

FATHER; She's invited practically the entire South Side.

WALTER: That's Mama…

FATHER: Her whole chapter's in on it.

WALTER: And you're footing the bill

FATHER Your mother thinks money grows on trees.
(beat) Here she is.

MOTHER: Walter? Everything in the world's happening right now. I can't get over it. The Links cotillion. We're giving five scholarships this year. Five. Meet our quota. Add a new one every year. **(beat)** Your mother's the president, darling. **(soft laughter)** And she's layin down the law. **(to an imaginary group)** Either sell those tickets, ladies, or get out your checkbooks.

WALTER: Hi Mama.

MOTHER: How have you been? I'm so worried about you.

(Doesn't answer. Walter is looking around for Etta.)

MOTHER: Walter?

WALTER: Fine. Just fine.

(still looking around)

MOTHER: I'm on my way to my hair appt…If they don't sell their tickets…They'll eat every single one of 'em. … Yes ma'am, 25 tickets a piece. We mean business. None of this laazzin' around. Getting up late. Wearin your nightgown all day. Uhuh.Walter? I'm so worried about you.

(Etta enters from the side in pajamas.)

MOTHER: You'll be home in time for the cotillion, won't you?

(Etta drops pots and pans. loud crash. hurriedly tries to pick things up.)

MOTHER: What's that noise?

WALTER: Nothing. **(Etta looks up quickly.)** Just nothing. I mean I'm cookin' breakfast.

MOTHER: Breakfast? It's one o'clock.

WALTER: I mean lunch.

(Etta is tugging on Walter, grabbing him around the waist. Bumps into the chair.)

MOTHER: Walter, is that you? I bet you haven't heard a word I said. You'll be home in time, won't you? Your dad wants you here with the other Kappas.

WALTER: Dad? He's fine. Won't bother him a bit.

MOTHER: Oh yes, it will. He wants you here. You know those Kappas. If you'd gone to dental school like your father, you'd be sittin' pretty by now. Walter, you need to settle down. (**long pause**) Walter? (**silence**) (**Walter trying to figure out what Etta's doing**) He's a million miles away. You'd better talk to your boy. Tell him! I 'm not doing this just for a song and a dance. His mother's worked her fingers to the bone.

(Noise in the background. Walter's mother is crying and fussing.)

FATHER: Here, let me have that phone. (**beat**) Your mother's over here crying. Said you weren't listening to her. Said you don't care about how hard she's worked. You know your mother. Won't take <u>no</u> for an answer. Straighten up and fly right, Walter, or she just might be standing at your door. (**beat**) I'm expecting to see you here on Saturday. I know it's not much compared to all the things you've been doing down South, but it means a lot to your mother. So don't let her down. (**loud click**)

(They're sitting at the table. Etta is still in her pajamas.)

WALTER: She's on a mission.

ETTA: Who? Your mother?

WALTER: When she gets going, you better move out of her way. You and my mother.

ETTA: Me?

WALTER: From that first day we met, you knew where you were headed.

ETTA: I have no idea what you're talking about.

WALTER: You were on a mission.

ETTA: Me? On a mission? Walter, I was facing cultural chaos. To pledge or not to pledge. Go. Stay. So many directions. It's enough to drive you crazy. I had to move out. Too much music. Too many songs. First one then the other. Not just two or three. A million. John Cage or Muddy Waters. Muddy Waters or Johnny Mathis. I don't even like Johnny Mathis. It's like a crazy quilt. So many I can't see straight. Is that how it's supposed to be? I was telling this prof of mine that I was really into New Music. John Cage. He was stunned. He'd heard about Cage. Knew he was on campus. Anyway, he wanted to know why I hadn't turned the paper in on time. I said it was because I was really into New Music and I was going to all these concerts in this big round house. He was so oblivious. Said "That's fine, but I'm still marking you down. And by the way, before you get in to Cage, better listen to a little Tchaikovsky, start with your foundation and work your way up." Tchaikovsky!

WALTER: What's wrong with Tchaikovsky?

ETTA: Tchaikovsky? I mean I like Tchaikovsky…he's okay. (gets close to Walter) So I'm walking out the door to his office and he stops me, looks me straight in the eye, pats my hand like this, says " Dearie," he calls me "Dearie," first Tchaikovsky, then you can work your way up to Beethoven, Strauss, Copland, then maybe Cage. Tchaikovsky? Nothing's wrong with Tchaikovsky. Everybody's heard of him. That's all.

WALTER: We were at this meeting together. Me and this white dude---Harvey---that's right, Harvey. We were talking about *Goodbye, Columbus*. I said that's not the way Roth talks about it. So he says "How do you know about

Philip Roth." What the hell? How do I know about Philip Roth? Like it was some state secret! A state secret! **(louder)** Me? I've been asleep. Catching zz's for the last 10, no 20 years. In a coma and I just woke up. **(starts to growl at Etta. claws. She laughs.**) Lord ha mercy.

ETTA: Rise and shine! It's 1963.

WALTER: Bout to miss my bus. Where's my lunch pail? Mr. Charlie gon' tear me up.

ETTA: They'll never going to believe you know anything.

WALTER: They? Who's they?

ETTA: You know who "they" is.

WALTER They.

(Walter and Etta embrace.)

ETTA: Walter. I'm the Lone Ranger, fighting this all on my own. Solo. Everywhere I go, I'm the only one.

WALTER: Going to concerts on Sunday afternoon, a couple during the week. **(sings)** "Hi Yo, Hi Yo Silver."

ETTA: It happens to me all the time. There I am. Me and this room full of white people.

WALTER: Etta against the world. She dares to go to John Cage concerts.

ETTA: John Cage? Did you know the Campus Blues Society brought in Muddy Waters? Doesn't matter. I'm still the solo act. Just this oddball showing up.

WALTER: Looking for culture with a capital C. I don't know how you do it, Etta.

ETTA: You try showing up uninvited. See how you like it. You don't know what it's like to be left out of things!

WALTER: Look, Etta, women are doing a lot down South. Going door to door. Showing up at the meetings.

ETTA: You don't understand anything about me. Not one single thing. I'm not in Mississippi. I'm in Champaign-Urbana. I'm not like the women down there. I can just see it, while they're doing the chores like good little girls, making coffee, fixing sandwiches, you're handling all the manly things. I'm not the Avon lady. Okay? Going door to door. What's that got to do with me?

(Frank knocks on the door or yells out from offstage.)

FRANK: Brother Daniels!

(Etta ducks offstage, hurriedly, frightened.)

FRANK: Hey Brother Daniels, you playin' at the Elks tonight?

WALTER: Man, it's crunch time. **(points to stack of papers)** Gotta hit the books. Take care of some things before I cut outta here. **(They bond.)** Semester's almost over and my thesis is due.

(Frank picks up stack of papers. Holds some of them up.)

WALTER: Copies of the State of Mississippi Constitution. Had to run all these off. Never even took a course on it, but I'm teachin' school. (**holds up copy**) Interpretation to the satisfaction of the registrar.

FRANK: You going back?

(**Walter darts for the record player. We hear *Kind of Blue*. Frank is digging Miles.**)

FRANK: When I was little, I couldn't wait for summer to come, so I could go down South. My Uncle Pack, big time Sigma man, he'd come up and get me. Uncle Pack Up And Go. That's what we used to call him. We wouldn't leave 'til about 9 at night. Never would drive in the daytime. Wodden't but ten years old. Shoulda seen me. Dancing in circles. So happy to be going down home. He'd put my suitcase in his trunk. Turn on the radio. Real loud. Pack Up and Go. Saturday night. Said he grew up listening to Gran Ol' Opry. On the way down, he'd always stop for gas. First he'd ask to use the rest room. Real polite. If they said no, he'd look 'em right in the eye. Bold like. Point to the hose. Say "Pull it out!" And off we'd drive.

WALTER: Your Uncle Pack was one…

FRANK: …bad man. (**nods in agreement.**) Doin' 80. Singing. Hmp. Like he was on the Opry. Used to be that's all you heard down there.
(**Etta comes back out, wearing a robe over her pajamas.**)

FRANK: Now, they're all dancin' to Randy's. Randy's Record Shop. (**dances over to Etta**) Brother Daniels, you must have that magic touch. Never could get her to talk to me. Miss Thing.

(Walter doesn't say anything. laughs nervously.)

FRANK: Miss Seditty. Can't even say hello.

ETTA: Frank, be quiet.

FRANK: Oops. Outer space. Calling outer space. Hey! Frank to Mars. Frank to Mars…**(Walter breaks it up.)**

WALTER: Let's bring it back to earth! I'm on my way down South, Brother Smith, getting ready to register people to vote.

FRANK: SNCC? Your folks? They'd get in an argument with a street light.

(Etta laughs.)

WALTER: You oughta try it.

FRANK: OhOh. Brother Daniels, man, you're tryin' to blow my cover.

WALTER: You have to keep things cool, right?

FRANK: That's right.

WALTER: How you gonna do that, huh? Stay cool, keep it all together, when the world's so crazy. Camus calls it absurd. You ever read Camus? No. You just know what they say about us on the radio. You know how they talk about us, don't you? **(beat)** Everybody's jumpin' on SNCC.

(Frank waves his hands in apology.)

FRANK: Didn't mean to get on your case, Brother Daniels. All this, it's over my head. You like to talk that talk. Philosophize. Camus, Ghandi. Heavy stuff. Deep.

WALTER: You got it all wrong, Brother Smith. It's not that deep. One week I talked to 100 people. Had to take a survey too. Goes like this. Vote won't be counted, not interested, don't have time to discuss the election, politicians going to do whatever they want. Next street: Wants time to think it over, been advised not to. All in all 10 agreed to register, 3 actually showed up, and those three left when the sheriff pointed his rifle **(imitates sheriff)**You keep going back again and again. Same people. Same house. You can't stop. You pick 'em up. Say "I'll go with you. I'll give you a ride." It's like a juggling act. How many plates can you keep spinning at once? **(Walter goes over and picks up some of the dishes that Etta dropped. A quick glare at Etta.)**

FRANK: That's okay for you. You can dig it. Me. I'm more hands on. Lady's man. **(to Etta)** Hey, and he's doing better than me in that category too.

(Walter picks up a big stack of paper. Hands it to Frank. Frank is a little embarrassed. Waves him away.)

WALTER: This woman took the registration test 11 times before they let her pass it. **(to Frank, angry)** Then you get to the hard part. You know about school. (shouts) About trick questions. **(yells)** THIS IS A TEST! How many seeds in a watermelon?!! How many bubbles on a bar of soap?!! Things anybody outta know!!!!!

(Frank waves Walter away, then walks to door.)

FRANK: Man, those dudes ain't playin'. You could get hurt doin' that stuff.

WALTER: You can get hurt anywhere, Brother Smith. On the job, at school. Never know when.

FRANK: (**They embrace and do improvisation with bonding. Frank heads towards door.**) Pack up and go! (**beat**) Tryna look out for my sand.

WALTER: I know, man. I know you well. I know you got my back.

(They embrace again. Frank leaves. Etta and Walter are alone.)

ETTA: Counting watermelon seeds. That's a good trick. They like that, don't they? When we moved to Chicago, my mother saw this big billboard with this little black child, big eyes, wearing a big straw hat , eating a humongous piece of watermelon. She never took another bite. (**beat**) Monica says I'm whitey-white. I'm not. Or maybe I am. She says I like white folks. Greys. I'm trying to get a handle on this. On what it means to be white. I wouldn't have the slightest idea. That's the great thing about John Cage. He doesn't care about any of it. Black. White. He's so experimental.

WALTER: You kiss like a white girl.

ETTA: How would you know???!!!!

WALTER: Cut the sophistication , Virgin Mary.

ETTA: I am not. I was not.

WALTER: When I met you, you were. You were one.

ETTA: Was not. That was only with music. I've been around!

WALTER: To a concert on campus.

ETTA: It wasn't on campus. It was off campus.

WALTER: You and 200 music lovers.

ETTA: At a private residence.

WALTER: Jammed in there like a can of sardines. Sounds like an orgy to me. (**says to the air**) All that stuff about being a musical virgin. I should've known. She's been perimenting…melodically.

ETTA: Look who's talking. Experimenting, huh? Oh and by the way, how come you know so much about kissing white girls?

WALTER: I'll be sure to tell you about it. Some day.

(***Misty* up and under. They start to dance.**)

ETTA: Poor little me. In the dark till I met you. You'd like to think that, wouldn't you? Sir Walter, rides in on his horse. Teaches the little dope the ropes. I've had plenty of experience. Plentee of it.

WALTER: Like?

ETTA: Like none of your business.. I'd bore you, Walter. Really, I would. One tedious escapade after the next. (**yawns**)

(Walter starts to fishing around for a station. Finds one. Then they start to dance to *Misty*. Lights fade. They're both in pajamas.)

ACT TWO SCENE TWO

(In Walter's apartment. Walter enters. Etta is sitting on the bed. Walter is wearing an undershirt and pajama bottoms. Etta is in pjs.)

ETTA: Romance. That's what I loved.

WALTER: Loved?

ETTA: Romance, Walter, I loved romance.

WALTER: **(holds her)** Past tense?

ETTA: I was in high school. All those books at the library. **(hugs Walter)** I had a plan. Grab a big stack. Shellabarger, Slaughter, Yerby. The first thing I'd do. Flip through. Look for the good parts.

WALTER: The good parts.

(Walter is exploring her body.)

WALTER: **(grabs her)** I caught her! She was cheating.

ETTA: Not on the heavy stuff….Dostoyevsky. That stuff. You read that all the way through.

WALTER: Absolutely no cheating.

ETTA: Oh I don't know…Shellabarger, Slaughter, Yerby. The first thing you do. Flip through. Look for the good parts.

WALTER: **(continues to explore her)** Not sure what you mean….I'm a little confused.

ETTA: Oh you know the good parts. When they "melt togther" Become one. Stuff like that. Then I go right to the last page. See how it ends. If there's a lot of tussling and tugging and sighing. Whoa! That's the book for me.

(They dive together on the bed. Etta props herself up on the pillow.)

I was a pretty fast reader. Maybe it's because I skipped the long boring parts, crossing the Potomac, a five day car trip with the general staff, a discussion of the geography of the Alps, **(Walter is exploring her.)** Boring. Boring Boring.

(They embrace. Walter jumps up, goes to the table, comes back with a package wrapped in mailing paper. Carefully opens it. Takes out a music box. Winds it gently.)

WALTER: Every day. When you open it….

ETTA: *Stardust.* It's playing *Stardust.*

WALTER: When you open it…Etta… Think about me.

ETTA: **(long pause)** You're going back down there? Aren't you?

WALTER: You knew that.

ETTA: You're leaving again.

WALTER: Think about me when you open this. **(She opens it again. It starts to play.)**

ETTA: I don't want you to go.

is Walter an existential?

WALTER: Have to.

ETTA: Why? I know you, Walter, you're just off on your big crusade. Why? You're not responsible for every black man in America.

WALTER: You think I woke up one day. **(Drum roll. Walter pounds on whatever's available, pots, pans, anything,)**

Said this is what I have to do. Go git Walter. Call his house. Nobody told me I had to. I don't have to. Understand? You think I'm so brave? You just don't get it, do you?

(Walter is moving around at first.) Remember Larry? That class I told you about? Etta? You wanna know what really happened? I was in chemistry class. Sittin' right next to Larry. We were playin' with that stuff, <u>together</u>. That's right. I was in on it too. **(deep bitter laugh)** The two of us were mixin' and pourin', back and forth. **(uses his hands)** When the fumes started to rise up, I was smart, jumped right under the table. I knew something was wrong. Poor old Larry didn't know what to do. My boy leaned over, right into it. Like he was watching a magic show. I never said a word. Never said Larry, move out of the way. Under here. With me! I was too busy looking out for number one. Boom. It went off, exploded, right in Larry's face.

ETTA: Now I get it.

WALTER You do? Every time I go home. I go see Larry. He quizzes me. Wants to know where I've been.

ETTA: I get it. You think it's your fault. You're responsible. You're the reason Larry can't see. Well, you're not. Okay, he's blind. But it's not because of you, Walter. **(Walter turns away.)** It's not your fault. Please, please stay here with me. You don't have to go back there. You can stay here with me. No more arguing all the time. I'll make you happy, Walter. I will.

(Etta is fiddling with the music box.)

WALTER: Etta, why can't you understand this. I can't stay. I can't turn my back on everything I've worked for.

(Etta throws down the music box.)

WALTER: **(angry)** You broke it.

ETTA: I didn't mean to. I do like it. I didn't say I didn't. I mean I do like it. I do, Walter. I do. It's lovely.

(Music here---Miles Davis---*Blue and Green*. They move close to each other.

WALTER: How do I make you understand this? It's not about me, about what I want personally. When I got into this, I agreed on some things, Etta.

ETTA: Rules. **(shakes her head)**

WALTER: No rules. No results.

ETTA: Rules. That's the great thing about art, art with a capital A. You experiment! Go wild. Push the envelope. Run. Walk. Leap. Highs. Lows. It's not about right. Wrong. Politics---all that stuff. I was put here for one thing—to live my own life the way I want to live it. My life. My music. When I look in the mirror every morning. Know what I see? Etta! On the way to another wild ride. John Cage rubbing a Kleenex on the microphone. And when I walk out that door. Who knows what's gonna happen. Life! It's up for grabs. It's about my individuality. I don't want any part of your rules. Lock step. Military. Ten shun. That's why I left the house. All the rules. Wear this. Don't wear that. Yes, big sister. No, big sister. I was fenced in, Walter. Fenced in. I'm an individual. I need my 'things…my music, my books, my life, Walter, my life.

(Walter moves away.)

ETTA: (overlapping) And I want to live it. **(beat)** Please stay here with me. Please, Walter. I'll make you happy. Happier than you could ever be down there.

WALTER: Etta. **(shaking his head)** Etta. Look, I can't live my life just to suit you!

ETTA: You don't have to. I'll do whatever you want. I will.

WALTER: Miss Opposite?

ETTA: Okay, I won't. Maybe I will. Just don't leave, Walter.

WALTER: Do you really think it's that easy? That I could throw it all away.

(Walter grabs a stack of papers and holds them up to her then tosses them on the floor.)

ETTA: **(mocking)** He's throwing it all away. **(beat)** I didn't throw it away, Walter. I gave it away. To you. I gave it to you. I'd been waiting for this. Waiting and waiting. All my experience, that was a big lie.

WALTER: Really?

ETTA: I wasn't just a virgin musically, you know.

WALTER: Is this the world traveler? Off on another escapade?

ETTA: You're the first. **(beat)** I didn't know what I was doing. I was scared…

WALTER: Wait a minute, Etta. You were begging me.

ETTA: Me? You were begging me.

WALTER: Etta, you were falling all over me. "Walter, we could stay here and study…catch up on things. I'll show you my City Lights."

ETTA: I think they call that being educational.

WALTER: Hah! You were like an invasion----from Mars. "Give it up, Walter." You want me to give it up. Everything I've fought for? To play doctor two or three times a day.

ETTA: Hah! Play doctor? I can't….believe…Play doctor? Is that all this means to you?

WALTER: You think this is easy, Etta. You know I don't want to go. I don't want to leave you. Not now.

ETTA: But you have to play by the rules, all your great rules.

WALTER: Look, Etta, I don't make the rules. They're not mine to break. Even if I could, like some kind of king on a throne, it just wouldn't be right.

ETTA: Playing doctor. Is that all it meant to you? Playing doctor. Then go on Mr. High and Mighty, Mr. Self Righteous. Leave me here. Go off and fight your great crusade. Go on. Keep running of copies of the Mississippi constitution. Who's gonna read it anyway. You and…oh yeh. Larry. That's right. Nobody else. (beat)Except, Larry, wait a minute, that's right. Larry can't see. (beat)

(Walter turns away. Etta picks up the music box and runs towards him.)

Go on say it. Say I'm a selfish brat. A shallow, superficial, inconsequential apolitical fun loving….fool. **(beat)** You make me feel so guilty.

(Walter shuts down, turns away.)

ETTA: Walter! I'm sorry.

(Still holding the music box, Etta slumps in her chair.)

FADEOUT

ACT TWO SCENE THREE

(Monica, Shirley and Feezie at the Pi Lambda house. Duckwalking. Low light.)

SOROR BANKS: Let's hear it! From the top!

(They sing as they duckwalk.)

FEEZIE, MONICA and SHIRLEY: Alpha Beta Gamma Delta Epsilon Zeta Eta Theta Iota Kappa Lambda Mu Nu Xi and Omicron. Pi Rho Sigma Tau. Upsilon

SOROR BANKS: (over the top) You're almost there!

FEEZIE, MONICA and SHIRLEY: Phi Chi Psi and Omega.

(Feezie is down on the floor. Shirley pulls her up.)

SHIRLEY: Stick with it, Feezie.

MONICA: You can do it.

FEEZIE: Water. Water.

SOROR BANKS: One more time! Half a round.

FEEZIE, MONICA and SHIRLEY: Alpha Beta Gamma Delta Epsilon Zeta Eta Theta Iota Kappa Lambda Mu Nu Xi

SOROR BANKS: In unison!

FEEZIE, MONICA and SHIRLEY: Stronger and stronger. Girls no longer. Pi Lambda women. Stronger and stronger. Girls no longer. Girls no longer. Pi Lambda women. Stronger and Stronger.

SOROR BANKS: Keep going. Pi! **Beats out rhythm.** Hit it!

(They shout out digits of pi:)
3.145926
5358979
3238462

FEEZIE: **(as they march offstage)** And so on.

ACT TWO SCENE FOUR

(A few days later. Etta is at Walter's apartment. He calls her on the phone.)

ETTA: Hello

WALTER: (**over the phone. far away.**) Hello? Hello?

ETTA: Walter? I was looking all over for you. When I got back from class you were gone. Gone. Just like that.

WALTER: Hey Etta, what's happenin'?

ETTA: "Hey Etta, what's happenin'." Just like that. Drop in. Drop out. Don't even say goodbye.

WALTER: You weren't exactly in a listening mood. Anyway, I had to ride down with Brother Frank. (**chuckles**) Pack Up and Go. Drove me down here, and he's headin' back to Chambana to pick up more supplies.

ETTA: You and Frank. Just a guy thing. Huh? You and your buddy. Fightin' the bad guys. (**beat**) I was going crazy looking for you. You couldn't even leave a note. "Bye Etta. It was nice knowing you. I'm going down South."

WALTER: I wanted to call you right away.

ETTA: I'm sure you had other things to do.

WALTER: They recognize our phone numbers, Etta. If I called out, they'd know where I was calling from. We're stayin' with this lady. We call her our mother in Greenwood. Big pot of mixed greens, hot water bread.

ETTA: I told my mother I was staying at the Y. If she finds out I've been staying at your place….

WALTER: Look , Etta, I can't talk all day. You know I'm not at home.

ETTA: If my mother comes down here , to see her little girl going to school in Champaign Urbana, Illinois, and finds me in your apartment she'll have a fit. I've got my reputation to think about. Maybe I'll come down there…to Greenwood.

WALTER: Etta, you know you're just talking.

ETTA: I can pack.

WALTER. No, you don't.

ETTA. Pack up and go.

WALTER: Uhuh.

ETTA: Won't take me but a minute.

WALTER: And come down here? Not you. Not you, Etta. That woman? The woman who took the test 11 times? They put her daughter in jail last night. They wanted her to strip. Do it with them.

(long silence)

WALTER: Etta? You still there? Etta?

ETTA: Did they?

WALTER: They tried. They tried everything. Everything they could to break her.

ETTA: She wouldn't let them.

WALTER: I could hear her screaming. Somebody would say "Cain't you say yessir, nigger, Cain't you say yessir, bitch." And she'd say I can, but I don't know you that well. And they'd beat her again, her screamin all the time. They beat her and beat her till she passed out. Blood everywhere. Saw them draggin' her back to her cell.

ETTA: You were in that jail.

WALTER: Yeh, and I was lucky to be there. Not out walking around for somebody's target practice. That's all you do down here. Go to jail. Social hour with the guards. Get out. Go in again.

ETTA: I'd pass out too. I'd never let them touch me. Never.

WALTER: Miss Opposite. Nobody's going to tell you what to do. Anything comes to mind you're out with it. You'd make those guards so mad. They'd kill you. You wouldn't last a minute down here.

ETTA: They'd never break me. Never.

WALTER: They beat her, Etta, and beat her…her own mother didn't know her …

ETTA: …her mother found out. I bet she's gonna sue 'em.

WALTER: Sue 'em! (**laughter**) Down here? They put her in jail too.

ETTA: You'd let them get away with that?

WALTER: *I'd* let them get away with that? Me, Walter, I'm down here all on my own. **(beat)** Etta, I'm a part of a group. SNCC . I'm not on my own. I can't just say: Here's what's right. You've been doing this all wrong. Nobody wants to hear that. Okay? I know you've analyzed everything under the sun, Etta. I believe that and maybe you do know more than anybody else, but that's just not the way it works. Not down here. I'm working with a whole lot of people. Every single one of them with a mind of their own. There's only one megaphone down here, Etta, and the man's holding it. And you know what's he's saying. "Nigger, get off the street."

(knock on the door)

ETTA: **(yells out)** Wait a minute.

(knock on the door again)

ETTA: Be right there.

(knock again.)

ETTA: Can I call you back?

WALTER: No!! You can't call me back! **(beat)** There, I said it. Etta! I didn't know how to leave you. How was I going to say no to Miss Opposite? That's why I left the way I did. Do you understand what I just said? Etta? Etta, I didn't want you to go. Not down here. I didn't want you to get hurt. Okay? Just love me, Etta. Okay? Just love me. That's enough. **(click)**

**(Long pause, then Etta puts phone down and goes to
door.)**

ETTA: Who's there?

FRANK: Frank

ETTA: Come on in.

(Frank enters. Etta looks surprised.)

FRANK: Had to come back. Pick up some things. Talk to
some people. Walter told me to stop by. See how you were
doing. I didn't necessarily want to go. Wodden't thinking
about it. Didn't cross my mind. Not at all. Not like I was a
little kid. Goin' down for the summer or somethin. **(beat)**
But I didn't want anybody to say I sent my brother to get
the job done because I was too scared to go myself.

ETTA: Walter. **(still holding the phone)** Said you were
making another run. Bringing in reinforcements.

FRANK: They could use em too. Ooh. I could feel it.
Didn't even have turn around. Feel those eyes trained on
me. Gotta move fast. I need a chair.

ETTA: Pack up and Go.

FRANK:. Yeh, Pack Up and Go, that's me. They're not
playing down there. Uh uh. They don't play. If I had a
dollar for every time I saw a rifle pointed at my head, **(puts
her hand to his head)** this close **(beat)** I'd be a rich man!

My Uncle Pack. You know he was at D-Day. Landed right there with the rest of em. Didn't live long enough to see this. Not this kinda stuff. He's gone now. Wonder what he woulda said? D-Day all over again. That's right.

(Frank sits down. Knock on the door. Jumps to his feet.)

ETTA: Who's there?

SHIRLEY: It's us.

(Etta opens door. Monica, Feezie, and Shirley enter.)

SHIRLEY: Don't look like the YWCA. Uhuh. Hey, girl. Couldn't take the heat.

FEEZIE: We're hidin' out.

SHIRLEY: The actives are looking for us.

FEEZIE: Whoo! It was getting to me.

SHIRLEY: Let's go find Etta. See what she's up to. Your mother called. Wanted to talk to Soror Banks about you coming back to the house. Your mama said you were stayin at the Y. **(Shirley looks around. Monica is looking around as if this is the first time she's been there.)**

ETTA: He's not here.

FEEZIE: Etta's mother. She's the mother of the church. A big time soror too. I wouldn't mess with her. No sirree.

MONICA: Nice place.

ETTA: Yeh.

MONICA: Hey, pledge sister. Thought you were through with us, didn't yah? **(hands her a sheet of paper)** Here. We gotta have this whole thing memorized by 10 pm tonight. You're the only one had it down.

(Frank moves closer to women.)

FRANK: Hey, ladies.

MONICA: **(looks around frantically. to Frank)** Where's Walter?

FRANK: Cleaning up Dodge, baby. Cleaning up Dodge.

ETTA: Mimeographing the Mississippi constitution.

FRANK: Cleaning up Dodge City. Hanging out in the pool halls , laundromat, wherever the folks go, we're there. Started out meetin' at the Elks. Till we commence to singing. Mayor said, get 'em outta there. Elks say no. You got the Elks on your side, you're good to go.

SHIRLEY: Feezie can sing all night.

FEEZIE: Don't talk about singin'. I never sang so much in my life.

FRANK: Feezie, I thought you were a voice major.

FEEZIE: Am, but you have to know when to stop, don't you?

FRANK: Uhuh, Not Uncle Frank, baby. He can't stop. He loves the action. It's in his blood.

SHIRLEY: Getting happy. I bet they could hear Frank singing all the way down the street. Frank was in church.

(Frank circles Monica. Looks her up and down. Monica pushes Frank away.)

SHIRLEY: **(to Frank)** You straightened them out didn't you.?

FRANK: That's right, baby. That's right.

(Monica doesn't act interested in what Frank's saying.)

FRANK: My boy the sheriff got right in my face. **(imitating sheriff)** "Nigger, we ain't going to have any more of this agitation 'round here. Niggers 'round here don't need to vote, so you and your damned buddy get out of here. Goddamn it Nigger! I'll give you one minute to get out of town or I'll kill you!

I say to myself. Let me see here. I think I'll give this a try. Me and Walter, we went down to this poolroom and I started talking to these boys. Told them they were going to be a part of a movement whether they knew it or not. They hooted and hollered. But you know they kept listening. Pretty soon they were going door to door, telling all their aunties and uncles they needed to register to vote. Didn't believe their vote would be counted. Went anyway. Ain't nothin to it.

(Frank starts to circle the women. They move back.)

FRANK: All the ladies want to check out the Kappa House. We just remodeled our lower level. Knotty pine.

MONICA: Not pine! **(The women laugh.)**

FRANK: That's right. Just like going to the Elks. You find a good Elks member, they're good at bailing you outta jail, loaning you their car. Help you keep your business straight. You ladies been down to the Elks haven't you? Showin' off your pledge line. Big strong line.

FEEZIE: We're hidin' out. Ooh . They're wearin' me out.

SHIRLEY: You? I duckwalked till my knees gave out. Fell right in the middle of the floor.

MONICA: You gotta be tough.

FRANK: You ladies need my good old fashion remedy, Kappa punch. Just a little sip. So nice and relaxed.

MONICA: **(to Feezie and Shirley)** Git on board, l'il children.

FRANK: Captain of the ship.

MONICA: Git on. That's right. They never taught us how to stop. It ain't easy. Never has been. Big sisters know how to make it hard, 'cause we got it hard. Way back when. It was hard. Still is. **(to Etta)** Once you're in, you don't leave.

FRANK: When you ladies get tired , completely exhausted and beside yourselves, come on over to the house and relax. Soft music. A cool beverage waiting just for you.

(Frank moves towards Monica. She throws her head in the air.)

FRANK: Oops. Pardon me. **(jumps out of her way)**

(The women laugh, all except Monica. She snaps everyone to attention.)

ETTA: **(to women)** I'll see you all later.

SHIRLEY: You think you're through with us? We're not leavin' that quick.

ETTA: I'm dropping out for awhile. I'll be back in a month or two.

SHIRLEY: A month or two?

ETTA: I'm headin' South.

(Frank turns to Etta quickly, stares sternly. The women look at each other worriedly, then leave.)

ACT TWO   SCENE FIVE

(Etta is on the phone to her mother.)

MOTHER: Going where?

ETTA: Down South. As soon as the semester's over.

MOTHER: With who?

ETTA: This group. I mean we've got family down there.

MOTHER: Down where?

ETTA: In Mississippi.

MOTHER: Mississippi? You've never been that far South in your life.

ETTA: Aunt Rose moved down there. **(beat)** You've been to Alabama. **(Mother moaning)** Mama, you got married at the Little Chapel.

MOTHER: Tuskegee? That's not the same thing. You wanna get married? You can get married right here in Chicago.

ETTA: Yes ma'am.

MOTHER: What group?

ETTA: SNCC.

MOTHER: You still talking to that boy? That boy…

ETTA: **(long pause)** Walter.

MOTHER: A nice young lady from Pi Lambda called me.

ETTA: I wonder who that was.

MOTHER: What was her name?

ETTA: Monica.

MOTHER: That's right. Monica. A nice young lady. Very polite. Said you weren't living at the Y like you said and she was worried about you. Concerned about your welfare. She said it's all over town about you leaving the house. **(beat)** About how you want to go down South.

ETTA: It's to register people to vote, Mama.

MOTHER: Alright. Alright. That's alright. Register people to vote. Good. That's good. Now listen. You give everything away. Who's gonna want you then? You're a nice girl from a good family. Don't let anybody tell you otherwise. I've seen this too many times. The young ladies at my church. Think they're sittin' pretty. Turn around. The boy's gone. Just like that.

ETTA: It's for SNCC.

MOTHER: SNCC. Alright. You could go down there for the summer. Get up in the morning. Have a nice breakfast with your Auntie. Go by folks you don't have to call first. Just swing by. Pop corn calls we used to call them. One right after the other. Breezy and cool. No fuss. Socializing, Etta. But that's not what you're gonna do..Is it? SNCC? I know you, Etta. You go down there. Slam bam. Summer's over. You're gone. Your Aunt Rose has to live there, Etta. Teach school. Go to the store. Everyday things you don't have to do. You go down there, start trouble, then leave, you'll leave it for them. They'll have to deal with it when you're gone.

ETTA: Yes ma'am.

MOTHER: I know you. Miss Opposite. I say one way, you're gone, the other way. Grab the stick shift, throw it in reverse.

ETTA: Mama....I'm...

MOTHER: Kinda nice, huh? Be the big rebel. Drive your mother crazy. I won't sleep a night while you're gone.**(beat)** Do you have any idea what you're getting yourself into? You know what they do to our girls down there?

ETTA: Mama, I'll look for a room at the Y...I will, Mama. I will. I love you so. Mama. You know how much I love you. Mama, I promise, I'll stay at the Y. I'll get all my things together. I'll move out of here. Today. Don't worry, please. Don't worry. I'll call right now. Trust me. I'll call the Y. I'll stay there. In one of those little rooms. Till...

MOTHER: Till?

ETTA: Till I get my things together.

MOTHER: Till you get your things together? : Well, well, my baby daughter. Your mama always spoiled you. Gave you whatever you wanted. Maybe that was wrong. You're gonna grow up fast. Real fast. **(beat)** Don't you let them put their hands on you, you hear? Don't turn back the clock. You show the world, darlin'. You're Mamie Bradshaw's daughter. **(beat)** Is it too late for you to go back to the sorority? Couldn't you just go through initiation then leave? **(beat)** Are you going? I asked you. Are you going down South?

ETTA: Yes ma'am.

ACT TWO SCENE SIX

(Etta finds Monica on the way to class.)

ETTA: Why couldn't you mind your own business?

MONICA: I was trying to look out for you.

ETTA: You take care of your business. I'll take care of mine.

MONICA: If you were the only one in the universe that might work.

ETTA: I can't believe it. You're worse than the FBI. My mother calls me. "Etta, this nice young lady from your sorority called me. Said you weren't staying at the Y." You called my mother.

MONICA: She needed to know.

ETTA: As if she's not worried enough. You have to go and…..

MONICA: Alright. Alright. I wanted you to come back. I wanted you to see what you're missing.

ETTA: You and me. Fighting all the time?

MONICA: Wasn't nothing to it.

ETTA: You miss that? **(beat)** You? Always on me about the West Side.

MONICA: Yeh, well I was sick of your high and mighty self. Miss Thing. You knew more about everything than anybody.

ETTA: Had too! "Hey Etta, Ghetto queen." I was sick of all your "The South Side this and the South Side that."

MONICA: Tonight we go over.

ETTA: Congratulations. I mean that.

MONICA: You could've been there.

ETTA: No, no (**Etta waves her away**) That's not for me.

MONICA: You're missing out on something. Something you can't get anywhere else.

ETTA: Maybe I am.

ACT TWO SCENE SEVEN

(Walter is calling his dad. Phone rings.)

FATHER: Hello

WALTER: Hey, Dad. How you doin'?

FATHER: Walter. I'm fine. Doin' fine. Your mother's got cotillion fever. Never saw anything like it.

WALTER: That's mama.

FATHER: Happens every year. Just like clockwork. Swears she's gonna take it easy. Hold off on all the heavy stuff. No over do. Every single time, she ends up wearin herself out. I'm tryin to stay out of her way. Thought I'd take in a little golf. Wouldn't mind a few rounds with you.

MOTHER: Is that Walter? Let me talk to him.

FATHER: Here she is.

MOTHER: Walter?

WALTER: Mama.

MOTHER: I hope you get here in time for your alterations. You know it's a new tux this year. (**beat**) Lordie. I've got so much to do.

WALTER: Mama…

MOTHER: Yes, Walter.

WALTER: I'm not going to make it to the cotillion.

MOTHER: Say what? I think we've got a bad connection.

WALTER: I said I'm not going to make it to the cotillion.

 MOTHER: What! Walter, I'm wearin' myself out trying to get things ready for you. All you have to do is come into town for the weekend. Try on your tux. Make a few calls. A few old friends. Young ladies. Meet some people. I want to show off my boy. Can't you see that?

WALTER: Mama, I met this girl.

MOTHER: Girl? Girl who? I don't know about any girl.

WALTER: A girl from Chicago.

MOTHER: What's her name?

WALTER: Etta.

MOTHER: And she's more important than my cotillion. I plan all year for this. One weekend. Walter. Just one weekend. (beat) What's her name again?

WALTER: Etta.

(A low moan)

WALTER: Etta. (beat) She's from the West Side.

(a louder moan)

MOTHER: I never know with you, Walter. I just never know. First you go down South. Then you're back. Doing

Lord knows what. You'd think you'd have some time for your own family. **(beat)** How'd you meet her?

WALTER: She's Greek. You know, we were at a party at the house. **(beat)** Just like you and dad. You were this pretty Spelman girl. On your way to class. The minute he saw you. Remember? You were walking one way. Thought he was going the other way. You told me. Whoa! He dropped his books right in front of you. Bent down to pick em up. Real slow. Like he was in a dream or something. "Is this an angel or a real live girl?" Swept him off his feet, didn't you? **(Mother's soft laughter)**

MOTHER: **(dejected)** And you can't come home?

WALTER: I can't, Mama.

MOTHER: Not even for the weekend?

WALTER: I can't, Mama. I'm in Greenwood now.